MW01165263

St. Mary Grade School
602 E. 8th Street
Dell Rapids, SD 57022

Nevada

by Patricia K. Kummer
Capstone Press
Geography Department

Consultant:
Jeffrey M. Kintop
State Archives Manager
Nevada State Library and Archives

CAPSTONE
HIGH/LOW BOOKS
an imprint of Capstone Press
Mankato, Minnesota

Capstone High/Low Books are published by Capstone Press
818 North Willow Street • Mankato, MN 56001
http://www.capstone-press.com

Library of Congress Cataloging-in-Publication Data
Kummer, Patricia K.
    Nevada/by Patricia K. Kummer; Capstone Press Geography Department.
        p. cm. — (One nation)
    Includes bibliographical references (p. 45) and index.
    Summary: An overview of the history, geography, people, and living conditions of
the state of Nevada.
    ISBN 0-7368-0022-0
    1. Nevada—Juvenile literature. [1. Nevada.] I. Capstone Press. Geography Dept.
II. Title. III. Series.
F841.3.K86 1999
979.3—dc21

                                                    98-3225
                                                    CIP
                                                    AC

Editorial Credits
Timothy W. Larson, editor; Timothy Halldin, cover designer and illustrator;
  Sheri Gosewisch, photo researcher

Photo Credits
Dembinsky Photo Assoc. Inc./Bob Sisk, 4 (bottom)
Dick James, 26
Kay Shaw Photography, 25
Maxine Cass, 30
One Mile Up Inc., 4 (top)
Photo Bank/David Carriere, 14
Photo Network/T.J. Florian, cover
Photophile, 34; Bachmann, 18; L.L.T. Rhodes, 20
Rainbow/Dan McCoy, 16; Jeff Greenberg, 22
Root Resources/Louise K. Broman, 5 (bottom)
Unicorn Stock Photos/John A. Schakel Jr., 29; H. Schmeiser, 36
Visuals Unlimited/McDaniel, 5 (top); Hal Beral, 6; Mark E. Gibson, 8;
  David Matherly, 10; Erwin C. "Bud" Nielson, 33

Table of Contents

Fast Facts about Nevada

State flag

Location: In the southwestern United States

Size: 110,567 square miles (286,369 square kilometers)

Population: 1,676,809 (U.S. Census Bureau, 1997 estimate)

Capital: Carson City

Date admitted to the Union: October 31, 1864; the 36th state

Mountain bluebird

Sagebrush

Largest cities: Las Vegas, Reno, Henderson, Sparks, North Las Vegas, Carson City, Elko, Boulder City, Fallon, Winnemucca

Nickname:
The Silver State
State animal:
Desert bighorn sheep
State bird:
Mountain bluebird
State flower:
Sagebrush
State tree:
Bristlecone pine

Bristlecone pine

State song: "Home Means Nevada" by Bertha Raffetto

Chapter 1

The City That Never Sleeps

Nearly 30 million tourists travel to Las Vegas, Nevada, each year. This number is more than three times the population of New York City. Tourists come to Las Vegas from all over the world to have fun.

Many adults visit Las Vegas to gamble in the city's casinos. Gamble means to place bets. The casinos are the main businesses in Las Vegas. They never close. For this reason, many people call Las Vegas the City That Never Sleeps.

Many people call Las Vegas the City That Never Sleeps.

Actors at the Treasure Island Hotel act out pirate
ship battles.

The Strip

Las Vegas' biggest casinos and hotels line Las
Vegas Boulevard. People call this street the
Strip. The Strip is three and one-half miles (5.6
kilometers) long. Colorful hotel and casino
signs light up the Strip day and night.

Nine of the largest hotels in the world are along the Strip. The MGM Grand is one of these hotels. It is the largest hotel in the world. There are 5,005 rooms in the MGM Grand.

Fun in Las Vegas

Only people who are 21 years old or older can gamble in Nevada. But there are activities for young people and families in Las Vegas. The MGM Grand Hotel has an amusement park. Actors at the Treasure Island Hotel act out pirate ship battles. Circus Circus Hotel has one of the world's largest circuses. Most hotels also host magic shows and musical shows.

Lied Discovery Children's Museum also is on the Strip. This is one of the largest children's museums in the United States. Visitors to the museum can learn what it is like to fly spacecraft. They also can find out what it is like to work at a TV station.

The Las Vegas Natural History Museum is located on the north end of the Strip. This museum's displays show the history of Nevada. Visitors can see dinosaur fossils and moving dinosaur models.

Chapter 2

The Land

Nevada is in the southwestern United States. Five states are Nevada's neighbors. Oregon and Idaho border Nevada to the north. Utah is Nevada's eastern neighbor. Arizona lies to the south. California borders Nevada to the west.

The land in Nevada is mountainous and dry. More than 150 mountain ranges stand in Nevada. Valleys with flat land lie between the mountain ranges. Many of these valleys are deserts.

The Great Basin Region

Most of Nevada lies within the Great Basin. Only Nevada's northeastern corner lies outside the Great Basin. The Wasatch Mountains in Idaho and Utah form the eastern border of the

The land in Nevada is mountainous and dry.

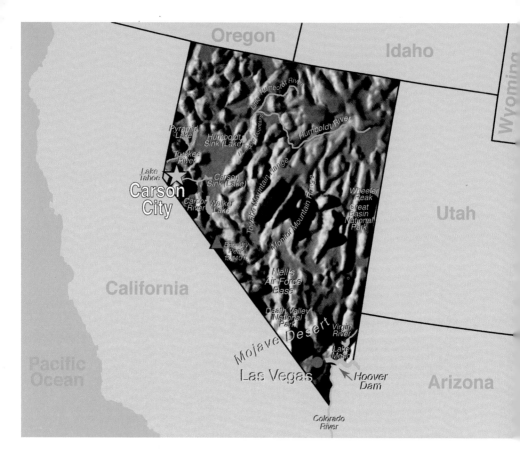

Great Basin. The Sierra Nevada in California and Nevada are the basin's western border. Mountain rivers and streams drain into the Great Basin. No water flows out of the region. Most of the water dries up quickly.

Mountain ranges lie within Nevada's Great Basin region. These include the Monitor Range, the Toiyabe Range, and the Humboldt Range.

Nevada's highest point is in the Great Basin region. Boundary Peak stands 13,140 feet (4,005 meters) above sea level. Sea level is the average surface level of the world's oceans. Boundary Peak is northwest of Dyer on the California border.

Ponderosa pine trees grow in the Great Basin region's mountains. Grasses and sagebrush grow in the region's valleys. Sagebrush is a plant with silvery green leaves and small, white flowers.

The Mojave Desert Region

Part of the Mojave Desert covers Nevada's southern tip. Nevada's lowest point is in this desert along the state's eastern edge. The land there is 470 feet (143 meters) above sea level.

Nevada's Mojave Desert region receives less than five inches (13 centimeters) of rain each year. But cactuses, sagebrush, and Joshua trees still grow in the area. Bobcats, bighorn sheep, and rattlesnakes live in the region.

Other Regions

Nevada's northeastern corner sits on the Columbia Plateau. The land there is high and mostly flat. Small shrubs and grasses grow in this area.

Lake Tahoe lies in the Sierra Nevada.

The Sierra Nevada region covers Nevada's west-central corner. But most of this mountain range stands in California. The Sierra Nevada form part of the Great Basin's western border.

Pine forests cover the slopes of the Sierra Nevada. Snowfields and glaciers lie in the higher areas of these mountains. A glacier is a large mass of slowly moving ice.

Rivers and Lakes

Some of Nevada's rivers flow into sinks. The sinks are areas of low land that often collect enough water to form shallow lakes. The Humbolt River drains into the Humboldt Sink. The Carson River flows into the Carson Sink.

The Colorado River flows along the eastern edge of Nevada's southern tip. Hoover Dam stands on the Colorado River near Boulder City. Water behind the dam forms Lake Mead.

Lake Tahoe lies in the Sierra Nevada. Lake Tahoe is the largest mountain lake in the United States. Other large Nevada lakes include Walker Lake and Pyramid Lake.

Climate

Nevada is the driest state in the United States. The lowlands receive only about nine inches (23 centimeters) of rain and snow each year.

Only the Sierra Nevada receive a great deal of moisture. As much as 500 inches (1,270 centimeters) of snow fall in these mountains each year.

Nevada's seasonal temperatures range from 32 degrees Fahrenheit (0 degrees Celsius) to more than 90 degrees Fahrenheit (32 degrees Celsius). Nevada's mountains have cooler temperatures.

Chapter 3

The People

Nevada is the fastest growing state in the United States. Nevada's population grew nearly 33 percent between 1990 and 1996. Nevada's warm, dry weather draws many people. Some people move to Nevada because it does not have a state income tax.

About 86 percent of Nevadans live in or near cities. Almost 80 percent of these people have homes near Las Vegas or Reno. Each month, about 5,000 people move to Las Vegas. Many new Nevadans come from California.

European Backgrounds
Today, about 84 percent of Nevadans have European backgrounds. Most of Nevada's early settlers came from other states.

About 86 percent of Nevadans live in or near cities.

About 7 percent of Nevadans are African Americans.

In the 1800s, thousands of U.S. settlers moved into Nevada. Their families originally came from Europe. Mormons came to Nevada from the area that is now Utah. A Mormon is a member of The Church of Jesus Christ of Latter-day Saints. Mormons founded the city of Genoa. Miners came to Nevada from California.

Other settlers came to Nevada directly from Europe. Irish and Italian people came to work in Nevada's silver mines. Germans built farms in the Carson River Valley. Basque people herded sheep in northern Nevada. Nevada's Basque people originally came from the Pyrenees Mountains in France and Spain.

Hispanic Americans

About 10 percent of Nevadans have Hispanic backgrounds. Nevada's early Hispanic American settlers came from Mexico during the 1800s. Other people with Hispanic backgrounds came later to look for gold and silver.

Today, Hispanic Nevadans have many backgrounds. Some have families who came from places such as Puerto Rico and Cuba. Other Hispanic people come to Nevada from South American countries.

African Americans

Few African Americans lived in Nevada until the 1930s. In 1931, the U.S. government and Nevada government started the Hoover Dam project. Many African Americans came to Nevada to take jobs building the dam.

Today, about 7 percent of Nevadans are African Americans. Most African Americans in

People from the Philippines make up Nevada's largest group of Asian Americans.

Nevada live and work in the Las Vegas area. Many other African Americans live in Henderson, Reno, and Carson City.

Asian Americans

About 3 percent of Nevadans are Asian Americans. Only Hawaii, California, and Washington have larger percentages of Asian

Americans. Asian Americans make up Nevada's fastest growing group of people.

In the 1860s, many people with Chinese backgrounds came to Nevada from other states. Some settlers came from China. Many Chinese settlers helped build railroads across the state. Today, Nevada's largest group of Asian Americans is from the Philippines.

Native Americans

Native Americans were the first people to settle the area that is now Nevada. Bannock, Paiute, Shoshone, and Washoe people were the largest groups living in the area. Illnesses brought by explorers and settlers killed many of these Native American people.

Today, about 1 percent of Nevadans are Native Americans. Paiute, Shoshone, and Washoe people are Nevada's largest Native American groups. Many Native Americans live in Las Vegas. Others live on reservations that they own and operate. The Paiute Pyramid Lake Reservation is the largest reservation in Nevada.

Chapter 4
Nevada History

Scientists believe Native Americans began living in the Great Basin region about 10,000 years ago. The region included the area that is now Nevada. The Native Americans left behind stone drawings called petroglyphs.

Other groups of Native Americans entered the area that is now Nevada about 1,000 years ago. The main groups included the Paiute, Shoshone, and Washoe people.

Spanish and Mexican Claims
Spain claimed the areas that are now Mexico and Nevada in the 1500s. But Spanish explorers did not enter the area that is now

Early Native Americans left behind stone drawings called petroglyphs.

Nevada until 1776. They were the first Europeans to arrive in the area.

In 1821, Mexico won its independence from Spain. Mexico took control of southwestern North America. This land included the area that is now Nevada. But few people from Mexico explored or settled the area.

Settlement and Statehood

In the 1840s, the United States fought Mexico for control of southwestern North America. This was the Mexican-American War (1846–1848). The United States won the war. It took control of what is now the southwestern United States. This region included the area that is now Nevada.

During the 1850s, some of the first U.S. settlers came to Nevada. Mormons from the Utah Territory built farms and founded Genoa, Nevada. About the same time, Peter O'Riley and Patrick McLaughlin discovered the Comstock Lode. They mined the large supply of ore near what is now Virginia City. Thousands of people moved into the area to look for gold and silver.

During the 1850s, people went down shafts like this one to mine the Comstock Lode.

During the early 1860s, the Northern states and the Southern states fought the Civil War (1861–1865). Many people who lived in the area that is now Nevada sided with the Northern states.

President Lincoln wanted the area that is now Nevada to join the United States. On October 31, 1864, Nevada became the 36th state. Carson City became Nevada's capital. About 15,000 people lived in the state.

The railroad linked Nevada with eastern and western states.

Growth in the New State

In the late 1860s, people settled northern and western Nevada. Miners discovered gold, silver, and lead in these regions. Ranchers also started cattle and sheep ranches there.

In 1869, the Central Pacific Railroad helped Nevada grow. The railroad linked Nevada with eastern and western states. The railroad opened Nevada to settlement. Trains carried Nevada's gold, silver, and livestock to markets in other parts of the country. By 1880, about 62,000 people lived in the state.

The 1880s were hard years for Nevadans. Most of the gold and silver in the Comstock Lode was gone. Unusually cold winters killed ranchers' cattle. Nearly 20,000 people left Nevada. Most of the people were miners and ranchers. By 1899, the state's population had dropped to about 42,000 people.

Silver and farming attracted 40,000 settlers to Nevada during the early 1900s. Miners found silver near Tonopah and gold near Goldfield. The Newlands Irrigation Project brought water to fields and made farming possible near Fallon.

World Wars and Depression

In 1917, the United States entered World War I (1914–1918). Nevadans fought in the war. Nevada's mining companies mined lead and copper for U.S. military factories.

Many Nevadans experienced hard times during the Great Depression (1929–1939). Miners and other workers lost their jobs. Farmers and ranchers could not afford to keep their land.

In 1931, the financial hard times eased in Nevada. The Nevada government made it legal to gamble. Many Nevadans took jobs with casinos. People came to Nevada to gamble. They spent money in the state's casinos, hotels, and stores. The U.S. government started the Hoover Dam project in 1931. Nevadans took jobs building the dam.

In 1941, the United States entered World War II (1939–1945). Many Nevadans joined the U.S. military. Nevada's ranchers raised beef to feed U.S. soldiers. Nevada's mining companies produced metals for military manufacturers.

Recent Growth
Since the 1960s, Nevada has been the fastest growing state in the United States. More than 1 million people have moved to Nevada. Many new businesses have opened. New gold mines have started production near Elko. Large ski resorts have opened around Lake Tahoe. People continue to build new homes, hotels, and casinos in Las Vegas and Reno.

Nevada's fast growth caused problems over the years. Crime increased in Nevada's largest

Nevadans helped build Hoover Dam.

cities. Las Vegas' schools became crowded. High populations, building projects, and growing businesses increased pollution in Nevada.

Nevada's government has been working on these problems. It has passed new laws to decrease crime. The government has provided money for new schools and more teachers. It also has worked to improve the environment throughout the state.

Chapter 5

Nevada Business

Service businesses are Nevada's most valuable businesses. Trade, tourism, and government are all service businesses. Tourism is the state's largest service business. More Nevadans work in tourism than in any other service business. Mining, manufacturing, and farming are other important Nevada businesses.

Service Businesses

Tourists spend nearly $28 billion in Nevada each year. They spend most of their money at the state's casinos, hotels, restaurants, and ski resorts.

Realty is one of Nevada's fastest growing service businesses. Realty companies rent or

Tourists spend money at Nevada's ski resorts.

sell land, buildings, and houses. Nevada's realty companies sell billions of dollars of property each year.

Thousands of Nevadans work for the U.S. government or the Nevada government. Some Nevadans work at Nellis Air Force Base. Others work in Nevada's parks and national forests.

Mining and Manufacturing

Nevada earns more than $3 billion each year from mining. Gold and silver are Nevada's most valuable mining products. Nevada produces more gold and silver than any other state. Oil, copper, and lead are other important mining products.

Nevada's main manufactured products include printed goods, computer parts, chemicals, and irrigation equipment. Most of Nevada's factories are in Las Vegas, Henderson, Reno, and Carson City.

Farming

Nevada's most valuable farm products are cattle, hogs, and sheep. There are only about 2,500 farms and ranches in Nevada. But farmers and

Irrigation equipment is one of Nevada's main manufactured products.

ranchers raise thousands of cattle, hogs, and sheep each year.

Hay is the leading crop in Nevada. Alfalfa seeds and garlic seeds are other important crops. Farmers in southeastern and western Nevada raise vegetables and fruits. Most farmers must use irrigation to grow their crops.

Chapter 6
Seeing the Sights

Nevada has five main areas. These areas are northern Nevada, central Nevada, south-central Nevada, southern Nevada, and western Nevada. Each area has its own landscape, activities, and events.

Northern Nevada

Nevadans call northern Nevada Cowboy Country. Winnemucca is the home of the Buckaroo Hall of Fame. Buckaroo is another word for cowboy. The hall of fame honors cowboys who worked on Nevada cattle ranches during the 1880s. Its displays show the history of cattle ranching in Nevada.

Nevadans call northern Nevada Cowboy Country.

Rhyolite is a ghost town in south-central Nevada.

Many large cattle ranches still operate in northern Nevada. Spur Cross Dude Ranch is south of Winnemucca. A dude ranch is a place where visitors can take part in cowboy life. Spur Cross is a working dude ranch. Visitors help ranch workers perform daily chores.

Central Nevada
Many Nevadans call central Nevada Pony Express Country. Pony Express riders rode

horses. They carried mail across central Nevada on horseback during the 1860s. Today, U.S. Highway 50 follows the route Pony Express riders once traveled.

Great Basin National Park is on the eastern end of U.S. Highway 50. Bristlecone pine trees grow in the park. They are among the oldest living things in the world. Some of them are 4,000 years old.

The old mining towns of Eureka and Austin are along U.S. Highway 50. Visitors tour buildings that people built during the 1800s. For example, Austin has the oldest Catholic church in the state. It was built in 1866.

South-central Nevada

Rhyolite is a ghost town in south-central Nevada. People left Rhyolite when nearby mines closed during the early 1900s. Visitors can explore some of the old buildings in this town.

Part of Death Valley National Park lies west of Rhyolite. Much of the park is colorful desert. Visitors can camp, hike, and bike in the park.

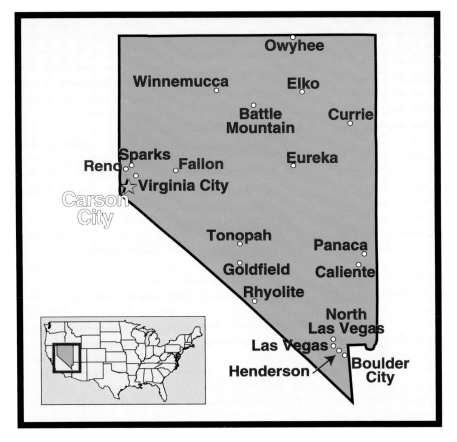

Southern Nevada

Las Vegas is in the middle of southern Nevada. The city is home to the Nevada State Museum and Historical Society and the University of Nevada. Many visitors tour the museum each year. The University of Nevada's sports teams are the Running Rebels. Thousands of fans attend Running Rebels men's basketball games.

Red Rock Canyon is west of Las Vegas in the Mojave Desert. The canyon's walls are red, orange, and yellow sandstone. Many visitors hike through the canyon. Creosote bushes grow in the canyon. Some scientists believe a few creosote bushes are more than 11,000 years old.

Western Nevada

Pyramid Lake is in far northwestern Nevada. In 1940, scientists found the preserved body of a man near this lake. Some scientists today believe the body is more than 9,000 years old.

Reno is south of Pyramid Lake. Many people visit Reno's casinos. Reno also is home to the National Automobile Museum. Visitors can see more than 200 cars and trucks there.

Carson City is south of Reno. The Nevada State Museum is there. The museum was once a U.S. mint. A mint is a place where people make coins. Visitors to the museum learn how workers made coins.

Lake Tahoe lies high in the Sierra Nevada east of Carson City. Campers, boaters, and swimmers enjoy outdoor activities there during summer. Visitors downhill ski on nearby mountain slopes during winter.

Nevada Time Line

About 8,000 B.C. — The first people arrive in the area that is now Nevada.

About A.D. 900–1150 — Shoshone, Paiute, and Washoe people are living in the area that is now Nevada.

1776 — Spanish priest Francisco Garcés becomes the first European to explore the area that is now Nevada.

1821 — Mexico wins its independence from Spain. It claims Spain's North American land that included what is now Nevada.

1846 — The United States and Mexico fight for control of southwestern North America during the Mexican-American War.

1848 — The United States gains control of the area that is now Nevada after winning the Mexican-American War.

1851 — Mormons from the Utah Territory found the city of Genoa.

1859 — Two miners discover the Comstock Lode near present-day Virginia City.

1864—Nevada becomes the 36th state.

1900–1902—Miners discover silver near Tonopah and gold near Goldfield.

1907—Workers complete the Newlands Irrigation Project.

1931—Nevada legalizes gambling.

1936—Workers complete Hoover Dam two years ahead of schedule.

1940—Scientists find the preserved body of a man near Pyramid Lake; scientists believe the body is more than 9,000 years old.

1951—The U.S. military begins testing nuclear weapons at the Nevada Test Site.

1954—People discover oil near Nye County.

1960s—Mining companies begin mining gold near Elko.

1986—The U.S. government establishes Great Basin National Park.

1997—Nevada's leaders work to stop Congress from making Yucca Mountain a nuclear waste dumping site.

Famous Nevadans

Andre Agassi (1970–) Tennis player; won the British championship at Wimbledon (1992), the U.S. Open (1994), and the Australian Open (1995); born in Las Vegas.

James E. Casey (1888–1983) Businessperson who founded United Parcel Service (UPS) in 1907; born in Candelaria.

Dat-So-La-Lee (1835?–1925) Washoe basket weaver whose baskets are on display at the Nevada State Museum; lived in Carson Valley.

Frankie Sue Del Papa (1949–) Lawyer and politician; she is Nevada's first female attorney general (1991–); born in Hawthorne.

Sarah Winnemucca Hopkins (1844?–1891) Activist for Native American rights; wrote *Life Among the Paiutes*; born near Humboldt Lake.

Greg LeMond (1961–) Bicyclist who won the World Championship (1983, 1989) and the Tour de France (1986, 1989, 1990); grew up in the Washoe Valley.

Pat Nixon (1912–1993) Teacher who served as first lady while her husband Richard Nixon was president of the United States (1969–1974); born in Ely.

Edna Purviance (1894–1958) Actress who starred with Charlie Chaplin in silent movies such as *The Kid* and *The Pilgrim*; born in Lovelace.

Wovoka (1858?–1932) Paiute holy man; he began the Ghost Dance religion among western tribes; followers of the Ghost Dance religion believe Native Americans will regain their land; born near Walker Lake.

Words to Know

casino (kuh-SEE-noh)—a place where adults gamble

glacier (GLAY-shur)—a large mass of slowly moving ice

Great Basin (GRAYT BAY-suhn)—the region of the United States between the Wasatch Mountains and the Sierra Nevada

irrigation (ihr-uh-GAY-shuhn)—a system of supplying water to fields

lode (LOHD)—a rich supply of ore in the ground

mint (MINT)—a place where people make coins

reservation (rez-ur-VAY-shuhn)—land owned and controlled by Native Americans

sink (SINGK)—an area of low land that collects water

To Learn More

Aylesworth, Thomas G., and Virginia L. Aylesworth. *The West: Arizona, Nevada, Utah.* Discovering America. New York: Chelsea House, 1995.

Doherty, Craig A., and Katherine M. Doherty. *Hoover Dam.* Building America. Woodbridge, Conn.: Blackbirch Press, 1995.

Fradin, Dennis B., and Judith Bloom Fradin. *Nevada.* From Sea to Shining Sea. Chicago: Children's Press, 1995.

Stone, Lynn M. *Ghost Towns.* Old America. Vero Beach, Fla.: Rourke Publications, 1993.

Thompson, Kathleen. *Nevada.* Portrait of America. Austin, Texas: Raintree Steck-Vaughn, 1996.

Internet Sites

Department of Museums, Library and Arts
http://www.clan.lib.nv.us

Excite Travel: Nevada, United States
http://city.net/countries/united_states/nevada

Hoover Dam
http://www.hooverdam.com

Travel.org—Nevada
http://travel.org/nevada.html

Vanishing Nevada
http://redsam.com/vanishing_nevada/index2.
  html

Welcome to Nevada
http://www.travelnevada.com/

Useful Addresses

Department of Museums, Library and Arts
100 North Stewart Street
Carson City, NV 89701-4285

Great Basin National Park
Highway 488
Baker, NV 89311

**Las Vegas Convention and Visitors
  Authority**
3150 Paradise Road
Las Vegas, NV 89109-9096

Lied Discovery Children's Museum
833 North Las Vegas Boulevard
Las Vegas, NV 89101

Nevada Tourism Commission
State Capital Complex
Carson City, NV 89710

Index